MAX
ADVENTURE TO ANCIENT GREECE

BY SAMANTHA METCALF

ILLUSTRATED BY IAN R. WARD

Second edition
Published in Great Britain in 2020 by:
Mysteries in Time Limited
info@mysteriesintime.co.uk

Copyright © 2016 Samantha Metcalf
The right of Samantha Metcalf to be identified as the author of this
work has been asserted

This book is a work of fiction and, except in the case of historical fact,
any resemblance to actual persons, living or dead, is purely coincidental

Illustrated by Ian R. Ward
www.ianrward.co.uk

All rights reserved. No part of this publication may be reproduced,
stored in a retrieval system, or transmitted in any form or by any means,
electronic, mechanical, photocopying, recording or otherwise, without the
prior permission in writing by the author

A catalogue record for this book is available from the British Library

ISBN 978-0-9935660-3-5

Hi! I'm Katie and I am 8 years old. Max is my older brother. He's really clever. He helps me with my home work when I'm stuck. He knows everything! But don't tell him I said that. He can get really annoying and know-it-all. He is always telling me stuff, but sometimes it's just too much. All I want is a simple answer, like 'yes' or 'no'. Instead, it's always 'maybe, because...' So annoying.

But he's not so bad. He always looks out for me. And we have fun playing games together.

I think my favourite thing is playing outside in any weather! I love going to the park, especially the adventure playground with the huge, curly slide. You can go really fast on that one, especially when you lie down! Mum hates it when I come home covered in mud, but I can't help it. The fun parts of the park are always the muddiest.

Hey, I'm Max and I'm 11. I love reading. I read comics and cartoons that make me laugh, and I read adventure stories about knights and castles, or pirates and buried treasure! Mum is always telling me I have an over-active imagination. I can't help it. My mind just starts picturing loads of weird stuff.

I also love solving puzzles. Grandpa always buys me books full of word-searches and crosswords. I like to time myself and see how fast I can solve them.

Katie is my younger sister. She is really energetic and fun to be around. She's really fast and sporty. I wish I could be as good as her at sports. But don't tell her I said that. She can also be really annoying, when she can't sit still for more than five minutes. And she doesn't stop talking!

But she's cool. I'm pleased she's my sister.

1

Max and Katie couldn't wait to get home. They had spent the afternoon at the local library with their grandfather and they both had four new adventures in their hands.

Katie's books were all different sizes and she was having problems carrying them. Each time Katie stopped to catch a falling book, Max walked straight into her back.

"Ow!" huffed Katie. "Watch where you're walking!"

"I am," replied Max grumpily, "but YOU keep walking in front of ME!"

Katie ignored him, and tried balancing the books on her head. When this worked, they both walked the rest of the short way home humming the same tune together.

Mum had seen them coming down the footpath and had pulled the front door open before they got there. Max and Katie left their grandfather and mum chatting in the kitchen and took their books upstairs.

Katie wobbled several times on the stairs, because she had no free hands to hold onto the banister, but eventually she reached the top step.

She was just lifting her left foot up to the landing, when Max yelled out so suddenly that Katie jumped and dropped all her books. She stamped her foot in anger and was about to shout at him, when he appeared at his bedroom door. The shout got stuck in her throat when she saw what he was holding: another Time Machine!

Katie didn't even bother picking up her dropped books; she left them lying messily on the landing and followed Max into his bedroom, closing the door carefully behind her.

They opened the box together, looking for the Mission Plan.

Where would they visit this time?

Mission Plan

Place: Ancient Greece
Date: 472 BC

Ancient Greece was divided into different
city states, each with its own king, army and
customs.

Two of the city states were always at war
with each other. One was led by King Theron,
the other by King Mikkos.

One day, King Theron's baby son was kidnapped.
He received a ransom note from his enemy,
King Mikkos. The only way to save his baby
son was to send soldiers to find him. But it
was an impossible task; every soldier he sent
was killed on the dangerous journey. It was
no use.

The King never saw his son again.

Task:

Can you help King Theron find his son? Can you
make peace between these two city states?

2

"Ancient Greece!" shrieked Katie.

She jumped up, pulled the door open and disappeared round the corner.

Max agreed that it was exciting, but maybe Katie was taking it a bit far.

However, her excitement made sense when she bounded back straight away with two of the library books she had left outside. She held them up in front of Max. "Ta-daaaa!"

Max smiled. He got up, picked up his own library books from his desk and held them up for her to see. He then copied his sister's high-pitched voice: "Ta-daaa!"

Strangely, they had both chosen Greek myths from the library today.

3

Max and Katie read the history book and learnt all about Ancient Greece. They learnt about how the Ancient Greeks worshipped lots of gods and goddesses. They saw examples of ancient orange and black pottery. They were surprised at how much the Ancient Greeks had influenced our modern way of life, from theatre and language, to architecture and the Olympics.

They then read their myths, excited to learn as much as they could.

When they had finished, Katie looked worried.

"I don't think I want to go to Ancient Greece," she said. "It sounds very dangerous."

Max looked surprised. "Why not? It's probably safer than Elizabethan London, and we survived that adventure!"

Katie looked down at the front covers of her

Greek myths and took a deep breath. "Because they had monsters with snakes for hair that could turn you to stone just by looking at you... and... and... and a beast with a bull's head that ate children and lived in a maze!"

Max stopped himself from laughing out loud by turning it into a cough. "But they're just myths, they're stories!" he explained. "They're not real! The Ancient Greeks told stories like this about their gods and goddesses. We're just going to an ancient country, nowhere magical!"

"But Time Travel is magical, and that exists!" she exclaimed.

Max rolled his eyes. "No, Time Travel is science." He turned away quickly, because he didn't believe what he was saying.

Magic? Monsters? Surely not...

4

They needed to get dressed like Ancient Greeks, but Grandpa was downstairs. This meant his fancy dress shop was closed.

Max had an idea. He went to the linen cupboard, where Mum keeps the clean bed sheets. He pulled out two large white sheets. He looked in Mum's sewing drawer and took a handful of safety pins.

Katie stood with her arms stretched out at her sides while Max folded and pinned the sheet around her. He then fastened a belt around her waist and stood back to admire his creation.

He then did the same for himself while looking in the mirror, while Katie used hair clips to pin her hair up on top of her head.

They looked the part now.

Max found the Time Travel sticker and they both stuck it onto their tunics. It had the symbol of a lightning bolt.

"It's the symbol of the god Zeus," explained Max. "It should keep us safe."

Katie didn't understand how a sticker could keep them safe, but for once didn't question her brother.

They both took a deep breath as Max programmed the Time Machine to take them back to Ancient Greece. They nodded to each other to show they were ready, and Katie pressed the large red button on the top of the Time Machine. The familiar buzzing began as they started their journey through time.

5

They arrived in Ancient Greece with a bump!

They had appeared out of thin air right in front of an angry-looking King on a throne. They heard a loud gasp and, when Max looked behind him, he saw a large crowd of men with shocked faces.

They were inside a large hall. The ground beneath their feet was white marble and there were enormous pillars holding up the ceiling. There were large clay pots dotted around the room. Katie thought she would definitely fit inside one with room to spare.

When they recovered from their surprise, two soldiers stepped forward and pointed their spears at Max and Katie's faces. Katie clung to Max and they both shrank back in fear.

The metal of the spear was almost touching their noses; Katie was going cross-eyed staring at the very sharp, very pointy tip.

Suddenly, the King gasped noisily. He jumped up
and waved the soldiers back. "Stop!" he yelled. "Don't
you see what they are wearing? Look!" He pointed
at the Time Travel sticker on Max's tunic. "They
wear the symbol of Zeus. They have been sent by the
mighty Zeus!"

A loud cheer erupted in the palace.

"You are our special guests," said the King
warmly to Max and Katie. "You are very welcome."

Max still hadn't recovered from the shock of

being threatened with a spear. He definitely didn't want that to happen again, so he decided to hurry things along. He cleared his throat and tried to keep his voice steady.

"You must be King Theron. We are here to help you find your son," he announced.

The King jumped up from his throne in excitement. "Excellent, excellent!" he cried. He looked up to the sky. "Thank you Zeus! I will never doubt you again!"

The king waved for two important-looking men with long grey beards to move, then beckoned for Max and Katie to sit down in their chairs next to his throne. "Let me show you the note we found in my son's empty cot."

The King clicked his fingers and a servant brought the note on a silver tray. The King held it out for Max and Katie to read.

Max and Katie finished reading the note.

To King Theron,

You have declared war on the wrong city state. You cannot defeat us. We have taken your son to show how strong and clever we are. The only way to prove that you are equal in strength, is by rescuing him from us. He has been taken to the middle of the maze at Knossos. You have one week only to save him.

From King Mikkos

Katie had heard of Knossos before, but couldn't remember where.

"There is no time to lose," said Max. "We don't know the way, so we will need some help."

"Of course," replied the King. He clicked his fingers again and two soldiers stepped forward. "These are my two most trusted guards, Akamas and Plades. They will help you in any way you need."

The soldiers bowed their heads to Max and Katie.

"Come on, we'll show you the way," said Akamas. The soldiers saluted the King, then led them out of the palace. The crowd cheered as they passed.

6

As soon as they left the palace, Max, Katie, Akamas and Plades visited the temple on the hill. The two soldiers prayed to the gods to keep them all safe on their journey. Max watched with interest. He was very pleased. They needed all the help they could get!

Next, they stopped at the market. While the two soldiers were busy buying bread and fruit for the journey, Katie hissed to get Max's attention.

"I've remembered why I know the city of Knossos," she whispered. "It's where the Minotaur lives."

Max looked blankly at her.

"The Minotaur lives in the middle of a maze. He is a very dangerous monster with a man's body and a bull's head," she explained. "And he eats children."

Max gulped. This could be a dangerous mission.

7

As soon as they reached a quiet street, the soldiers stopped and turned to Max and Katie.

"Are you sure you can help?" asked Akamas.

Max was surprised. "Yes, I think – er, I mean, yes! We can! Zeus sent us to help!"

"I hope you're right," replied the soldier gloomily. "This is the most dangerous journey in the whole of the land. There are many deadly obstacles on the way."

The second soldier nodded. "The only way we can all survive this journey, is if Zeus is on our side."

Max and Katie looked at each other in fear. Were they foolish to think that they could survive this journey?

8

They left the city walls and started their long journey towards Knossos.

They were walking along a narrow path in a valley, with steep cliffs reaching high above their heads. The sun was strong and they stopped to rest on the rocks. They agreed to take a break to drink some water and eat some bread.

All of a sudden, a terrible noise started echoing around them. High above their heads, small stones started falling down the cliffs, disturbed by the rumbling noise.

They all stood up, back to back, looking all around them. What could this noise be? It sounded like a frightening creature. Max started to imagine all sorts of ugly beasts.

At last, an army of scruffy men stepped into the valley before them. Max counted at least twenty of them. How would they get out of this? They were outnumbered.

"You are King Theron's people. You cannot pass through this valley," shouted the strongest of them. "We will count to ten. If you wish to live, then you must be gone before I reach zero."

"But these are messengers sent by Zeus!" shouted Plades. "You don't want to upset the mighty Zeus."

Unfortunately, this statement did not have the effect that Plades had hoped for. In fact, they all laughed. "Haha, then Zeus will help you run fast enough to escape from our spears!"

Max, Katie and the two soldiers turned and ran as quickly as they could back the way they had come.

They had just turned the corner, when the booming voice reached number one . They heard a whooshing noise getting louder. Just as they reached safety, a spear whizzed past Max's ear and landed with a thud, its point buried deep in the ground.

They all fell to the floor, catching their breath, happy to be in one piece.

"Phew, that was close," puffed Katie. "Which way now?"

Akamas looked at Katie with wide eyes.

"You don't understand. There's no other path to Knossos," he said. "We have failed. We cannot save Baby Heracles."

9

They all sat in silence, thinking about the poor baby trapped at the centre of a maze inside a walled city the other side of those angry villagers.

They all felt hopeless.

Suddenly, Katie had an idea.

She jumped up, pulled the spear out of the ground and ran over to the long grass by the side of the path. She used the sharp blade to cut several long blades of grass, some as long as her arm.

The others watched as Katie then stood on her tiptoes and reached up to pick a handful of red berries from a nearby tree.

She then pulled some moss from the ground.

Max scratched his head as he tried to work out what his sister was doing. He couldn't.

Katie brought the grass, berries and moss to where they were all sitting. She was clearly very excited.

"I have a plan!" she announced happily. "Come close, let me explain!"

They all leaned in and listened carefully.

As soon as Katie had finished explaining her plan, they all got to work.

The two soldiers rolled around in the dust and rubbed the grey dust all over their faces and hair.

Max did the same, but only on one half of his body and face. If you looked at him from the left, he looked normal; if you looked at him from the right, he was covered in grey dust!

Katie rubbed the green moss into her face to give her cheeks, chin and forehead a grass stain. She used tree sap to stick two red berries onto the ends of each long blade of grass. Max helped her attach the other ends of these blades of grass to her head using her hair clips.

"Are you sure this will work?" asked Akamas

nervously.

Katie smiled. "There's only one way to find out!"

The two soldiers tiptoed on through the narrow valley again and round the corner out of sight. Max and Katie heard them shout out in pain, then nothing. Max looked at Katie wide-eyed.

"I hope that was them acting their role, and not real pain," said Max.

10

It was now or never.

Max went on ahead, shouting as he turned the corner.

"No! Please don't!" he yelled. "Save yourselves!" He saw Akamas and Plades standing still there in front of him. They were frozen solid and covered in grey dust; they looked just like statues.

The angry villagers had appeared and held their spears up once again, although this time they seemed less confident. They looked from the unmoving soldiers to Max's crazed expression.

"Run! RUN!" screamed Max. "Run far away before she turns you to stone!"

"What...who?" asked the leader nervously.

"Medusa! The witch with snakes in her hair! Don't look at her eyes! If you do she will turn you to..."

At this point, Max turned to look behind him, where Katie had emerged waving her arms while cackling like an evil witch. Max turned his body around, so the dusty half was closer to the villagers. Then he froze to the spot. He was good at playing Musical Statues, so this was easy.

Katie threw her head back and roared at the sky.

The villagers looked from Max to the other soldiers, back to Max then to Katie. Katie slowly turned her head towards the villagers, keeping her eyes wide and staring. The villagers screamed in fear, dropped their spears and axes and ran as fast as they could back into the forest.

Max and the soldiers counted to ten in their heads, then unfroze. It had worked! They grinned at each other then quickly brushed themselves down. Katie pulled the fake snakes out of her hair then picked up an axe. "Let's go," she said. "They may come back."

11

The group continued on towards the city of Knossos. Their mood was much more joyful after their success at tricking the villagers.

"How on earth did you think that could work?!" asked Plades. "A witch called Medusa with snakes for hair who turns people into statues by looking at them. What a funny story!"

"I agree," said Akamas. "Your imagination is very strange indeed."

Max and Katie smiled at each other. They didn't explain that the idea came from an Ancient Greek myth.

They walked for several hours, but at last they arrived at the city walls. There was a very large gate with no handles on the outside. They tried pushing it, but it was locked. Max knocked on the gate and stepped back. Nothing.

They looked up and
along the wall. It was too
high and straight to climb.
There were soldiers on top
of the gate. They realised
they were being watched.

"You are King Theron's
men," shouted one. "You are not welcome here."

"We are here to make peace with your King," said Max.

The soldiers laughed at him. "Peace? That's the funniest
thing I've heard all week!" As soon as he had recovered
from his laughing fit, he stood straight. He suddenly

looked very
serious.

"Now leave,
or you will
be killed," he
snarled.

12

Max and Katie looked at each other. The colour had drained from their faces. Now what?

Akamas brought them to their senses. "Hurry, we have to move," he said. He led them away from the gate, where the soldiers had started to point their spears down at them.

They all ran to the safety of the forest, where they sat down to think.

"There's no hope now," said Katie. "Did you see how high those walls were? There's no way we could ever climb them."

"Definitely not," agreed Plades. "And those soldiers are expecting us. They will never let us in."

They all sat quietly, imagining the worst.

The sun was getting low in the sky and the forest was cool and shaded.

Suddenly, Max had an idea. "Katie, you really are

a genius!"

Katie looked up, confused. "Er, I'm pretty sure I didn't say anything…"

Max explained his plan. They all looked at him strangely, wondering if he actually believed it could work. He realised how far-fetched it sounded, but they had no other plan.

"It worked at Troy," he said. "It could work here too!"

The two soldiers looked at each other. "Troy? You mean this tricked people at the gates of Troy?"

"Yes!" smiled Max. He obviously didn't tell them that this, too, was possibly a myth.

The soldiers had a renewed sense of excitement at the possibility of getting past those laughing soldiers.

"Come on, help me collect as many bits of wood and long vines as possible!"

They all got to work.

As soon as they had a pile of logs, Max picked

up the axe that Katie had taken from the villagers. He started chopping the wood and carving it with Plades' knife. Max carved grooves into the wood, so it slid together and held without nails. Any other parts were tied together using vines.

Just as the sun was starting to set, they finished. They stepped back to admire their masterpiece.

They had built an enormous wooden horse with four wooden wheels at its base.

Akamas looked up at the darkening sky. "It's now or never," he said. "We wish you all the luck in Olympus. Be very careful. If they find you, they will arrest you. Or worse."

13

They all shook hands and got ready.

The horse was hollow. Max and Katie climbed inside the horse's belly through a trapdoor underneath. Once they were inside, Max slid the trapdoor into place. They knocked three times on the inside of the wood to signal they were ready, then they felt the horse move.

Akamas and Plades led the horse to the gates as agreed. They announced to the guards on the gate that this was their peace-offering.

"You have won," said Akamas. "Please accept this horse as a sign of our surrender."

They tapped the horse three times to signal secretly to the hidden Max and Katie that they were leaving, then walked away into the forest.

Max and Katie were on their own.

Now, they had to wait.

Max and Katie were not comfortable at all inside the horse's wooden belly. They were crouching down and their arms and legs were crooked. Katie's hair kept tickling Max's arm, and every time he twitched his arm, his elbow stuck into Katie's side.

"You're so annoying!" hissed Katie.

"Speak for yourself!" whispered Max back.

Katie tried to take her mind off her aching legs by thinking of something soft and fluffy. She imagined that the wooden horse was really a giant ice-cream mountain. Soon, she was fast asleep.

Somehow, Max also dozed off after a while.

Until, that is, they felt the ground move.

They woke with a start. There was nothing to hold on to, but they threw their arms out to steady themselves.

They were moving! They looked at each other with worried eyes.

Had the plan worked? Were they on their way into the walled city? Or had they snored too loudly and given the game away. Were they prisoners?

Either way, they were absolutely helpless.

They just had to wait.

And hope.

14

They listened carefully; they knew they were inside the walled city, because they had heard the large wooden gate creaking closed behind them, then a loud noise as it was locked. They felt themselves move a short distance, then stop.

"And you're sure they didn't get past you at the gate?" asked an anxious voice.

Max and Katie recognised the laughing guard's voice. "I'm sure," replied the guard confidently. "We didn't even open the gates. We spoke to them from above. They are probably dragging their pathetic feet back to King Theron as we speak!"

"I hope you're right," warned the older man. "I have heard rumours that Zeus is on their side."

"Don't worry, there is no possible way that they could get through those gates," assured the guard. "If you want me to check, I will go to the maze now."

15

They heard footsteps and voices fade away, then silence. They waited.

They had now been stopped for at least half an hour. All was quiet. They decided to open the trapdoor a little, to see if the coast was clear.

Max lifted it slowly, wincing at the creak it made. He felt beads of sweat dripping down from his forehead to the tip of his nose. His hands were slippery with sweat. He had to be careful not to drop the door onto the paved ground below.

Once open, he set it aside, then lowered his head through the gap. He was looking at the world upside-down, but could see they were safe.

It was dark. On the other side of the square, there was a large group of men with their backs to Max and Katie. They were listening to a man with a long beard speaking. Further along, there were actors in masks, with a small audience clapping and laughing.

Max lifted his head up-right, then lowered himself down through the trapdoor. He stood still for a moment, checking nobody had noticed him, then beckoned for Katie to follow. He helped her down, then replaced the trapdoor silently.

They both stretched their backs and wiggled their arms and legs to try to get feeling back. Katie had a numb foot that she was trying to bring feeling back to by doing a silly dance. Max turned his neck from side to side, making a loud click! He froze, worried that people would have noticed.

"I don't think it was loud enough for anyone else to hear!" whispered Katie as she giggled to herself.

They started to tiptoe away from the horse, then began to walk as normally as possible, like they were meant to be there.

"Now what?" asked Katie.

"Now we need to find the maze," replied Max. "Maybe it's inside the temple."

Katie pointed up the hill. "That must be the temple."

Max agreed. It was a large rectangular building with tall columns holding up the roof.

They walked quickly, but stopped in their tracks. They heard a laugh that they recognised. It belonged to the guard at the gate.

They had to hide before he recognised them.

16

They looked around desperately, hoping for a dark alley or a doorway to hide in. But there was nothing. Just walls and open space.

They could feel the panic start to rise, when Max spotted two masks lying on the step nearby. The group of actors were taking a break from performing.

Max picked up two of the masks and passed one to Katie. They had to think fast. They improvised.

"Whatever you do, you must never look at the evil Medusa in the eye!" boomed Max.

There was silence. A crowd was starting to gather around them. Katie looked round at the faces and realised with a stab of panic that the guard from the gate was one of them!

"I said... don't EVER look at Medusa in the eye!"

Katie understood what she had to do. "Oh?" she replied, trying to disguise her voice. "What would happen if I looked her in the eye?"

"You mean you don't know?" replied Max. He stepped back and threw his hands to his face in pretend horror and shock. "She would turn you to stone." He paused for dramatic effect. "FOREVER!"

Katie felt like she had to be just as loud and exaggerated. She fell to her knees and thumped the floor. "Noooo!" she wailed. "That's just awful! Stay away from the witch Medussssaaaaaa!"

Katie eventually stopped wailing and realised there was total silence in the square, except for the slight echo of her own voice ringing in her ears. You could have heard a pin drop.

Katie held her breath for what seemed hours. Was she too loud? Had the guard recognised her? Maybe the angry villagers had followed their footprints to the walled city and told this story. By the time Katie had decided that they were doomed, the crowd suddenly started clapping and cheering.

They couldn't believe it! They stood together and bowed. Max and Katie waited for the crowd to leave, but they kept clapping. And clapping. And clapping.

They couldn't remove the masks, so they just kept bowing. Just when they thought they couldn't go on any longer, a messenger ran up to the guard and whispered something in his ear. They guard looked shocked, then angry, then ran back down to the square. Back to where the wooden horse was.

The trapdoor must have been found.

They had to leave now.

17

The messenger went back up the hill. Max and Katie followed, keeping their distance, hoping the messenger would lead them to the maze. They hid in the shadows and watched him walk up to the entrance of a large cave.

"The entrance to the maze must be inside that cave!" whispered Max.

There were no guards near the entrance, no signs, nothing to announce that this was the place where the kidnapped baby was being held.

The guard looked around to check he wasn't being followed, then disappeared inside the cave.

They waited for nearly half an hour before the guard appeared again. He was whistling to himself as he marched past, swinging his arms and legs happily.

Max and Katie waited until he was out of sight before they talked.

"There must be other guards inside the cave, inside the maze," said Katie. "How on earth will we get past them?"

Max was also thinking. "I don't know," he said. "Is there anything in the Minotaur myth that could help us?"

Katie thought hard, but couldn't think of anything. She threw her hands in the air in frustration and sat down.

"No," she said sadly, putting her head in her hands. "There's just a beast inside the maze who eats children. This is no good, there's no hope!"

Max smiled. "Then let's make a Minotaur!"

They had passed a small farm along the path, and Max ran back to collect some materials. There was a large basket filled with feathers and pieces of wool. There were even some animal skins hanging up. He checked that the coast was clear, then took as much as he could carry.

Katie, meanwhile, had remembered another important part of the Minotaur myth: they needed a ball of wool to help them find their way out of the maze again. Katie remembered they had passed a child about her own age selling balls of wool from a basket, and ran to find him.

She suddenly realised she had nothing to give him in return. She had no Greek money! She offered him the axe that she had taken from the villagers, but instead of explaining herself, she lifted the axe for him to see.

Katie was standing above him, the light was behind her, so all the boy could see was the silhouette of the axe being raised above his head.

"Aaaaggghhhh!" he screamed, throwing his hands up to protect himself. He clearly thought his life was in danger and ran away.

Katie realised what had happened and called after him. "Hey, wait! I wasn't going to hurt you!"

But he was gone. He had, however, left the basket behind. She shrugged to herself, then took a ball of wool, leaving the axe in its place as payment.

Back at their meeting place, Max and Katie set to work. They used Katie's hair clips to fasten the animal skin round Max's shoulders. They then used more tree sap to stick some bits of wool and feathers to fill the gaps. They left gaps for his eyes and mouth, and Katie stepped back to admire their work.

They had done such a good job, that Katie actually shuddered at the sight.

"Let's go. Remember, stay behind me!" said Max.

They tiptoed to the entrance and waited. Soon, Max saw his chance. He leapt out and roared at a passer-by, who screamed and ran away terrified.

Having heard the scream, two guards came running out of the maze. Max and Katie were now hiding, so the guards ran right past them.

Max and Katie had to act fast. They slipped inside the cave. Katie had tied the loose end of the wool to a rock and was slowly unravelling it as they went. They walked slowly, partly to stay as quiet as possible, but also because Max couldn't see very well inside his mask.

They made a few wrong turns and found themselves at a dead end, but they could re-trace their steps thanks to the wool trail and try again.

Suddenly, Max stopped dead. He could hear voices up ahead.

Voices and a baby's cry.

18

Max was about to follow the voices, when Katie put her hand on Max's arm to stop him.

"What if… what if…" started Katie.

Max signalled for her to hurry up.

"What if there's a Minotaur there," she whispered. "A REAL one!"

"Well, he won't eat me because I'm a Minotaur too," replied Max. "You're in trouble though," he joked.

There was no time for Katie to get annoyed; at that very moment, the two guards appeared round the corner and saw Max and Katie. Max froze. He'd lifted his mask away from his mouth so he could speak to Katie, but it looked even more menacing, like he was leaning down over Katie.

Katie screamed, as they had planned, and Max roared as loudly as he could. He charged at the soldiers, who couldn't believe their eyes. They dropped their weapons and ran. They even ran the wrong way in fear. They would be lost for a while yet.

Max and Katie stepped forward and around the next corner of the maze. There in the middle, on a comfortable bed of blankets, was a baby.

Katie loved babies. She went straight over with a smile, but her smile froze on her face. She couldn't move. There was something in the baby's hands. There was something moving in the baby's hands.

It was a snake.

19

Max and Katie had to think.

They both ran back round the corner to where the soldiers had dropped their weapons. They picked them up and raced back to the baby, desperately hoping they weren't too late.

But something very strange had happened in the short time since they had turned away.

The baby was still gurgling and blowing bubbles. The snake was still in his hands.

But the snake was still.

It was no longer moving.

They carefully leaned forward.

The snake was dead.

The baby had killed it with its bare hands.

20

Max pushed the snake off the baby with the handle of the spear.

"Be careful," warned Katie.

Max made sure he didn't touch it with his bare hands, and kicked it into the corner. They were safe. Katie picked up the baby, who stared with wild eyes at Max. The baby's lower lip started to wobble. He was going to cry.

Max realised he was still wearing the Minotaur mask. He pulled it off his head just in time. The baby smiled.

They walked back out through the maze, winding the wool up as they went.

Outside, they came face to face with the guard from the gate.

They all stopped in their tracks.

The guard's mouth opened and closed like a

fish. He looked from Max to Katie to the baby in disbelief.

He was speechless. Max was looking around, trying to see the best way to run, when the guard did something surprising.

Max and Katie watched the guard remove his helmet and bow his head.

"You have achieved the impossible," he said. "You have faced terrible danger on your journey here, tricked your way inside our city walls, and even successfully found your way through the maze to this baby and back out in one piece."

The guard signalled for the other soldiers to step back.

"You are free to go," he said, stepping aside.

They walked down the hill towards the square, where they heard a large commotion near the gate.

The baby's father, King Theron, had arrived. Akamas and Plades had brought him.

21

They were all now inside the palace, where a feast was laid out. The whole town was invited for the celebration. There was beautiful music from the lyre players, the actors from the square were acting a play about an evil child-eating beast with a bull's head.

King Mikkos apologised to King Theron.

"I am so sorry, King Theron," he said with a bow.

"I would never have hurt your baby, I would have treated him like my own son. What can I give you to show you that I mean no harm?"

King Theron shook his head and smiled at his son. "I now have everything that is important to me."

They shook hands and agreed to be friends from now on. They were both tired of being at war.

Max and Katie were heroes. They had brought peace between the two city states.

Sadly, Max and Katie had to make their excuses and waved goodbye to their new friends.

They stepped out into the cool night air and looked up at the stars. Music drifted out and the atmosphere felt so dreamlike, they didn't even notice when the light swirled around them and transported them back to Max's bedroom.

"See, Katie? There were no monsters or magic in Ancient Greece!"

"I'm not sure," replied Katie seriously. "That baby

had super-human strength."

Katie's eyes fell on the library books on Max's floor.

"What was the baby's name?" she asked quietly.

"Hera... Heracle... Herc... something like that," replied Max.

"Heracles?" asked Katie, wide-eyed. She held up Max's library book.

Max's face drained of colour. "So, Heracles really was a strong baby," he said slowly. "That means... that means... surely not!"

"Maybe there was a real Minotaur somewhere in that maze," finished Katie.

Max shuddered. "Let's go to the park," he suggested. "There are definitely no monsters there!"

The End.

See you on our next adventure!

Also in the Mysteries in Time series:

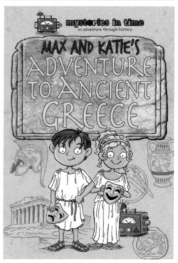

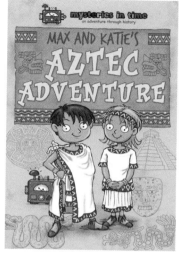